P9-CQW-208

SCOOBY-DOO!

THE FRIGHT AT ZOMBIE FARM

Stone Arch Books
A Capstone Imprint

You Choose Stories: Scooby-Doo
is published by Stone Arch Books,
A Capstone Imprint
1710 Roe Crest Drive
North Mankato, Minnesota 56003
www.capstonepub.com

Copyright © 2015 Hanna-Barbera.
SCOOBY-DOO and all related characters and elements
are trademarks of and © Hanna-Barbera.
WB SHIELD: ™ & © Warner Bros. Entertainment Inc.
(s15)

CAPS32625

Cataloging-in-Publication Data is available on the
Library of Congress website.
ISBN: 978-1-4342-9713-6 [Library Hardcover]
ISBN: 978-1-4342-9715-0 [Paperback]
ISBN: 978-1-4965-0213-1 [eBook]

Summary: When Scooby-Doo and the Mystery Inc.
gang visit their artist friend David at his farm in this
You Choose book, they find zombies instead.

Printed in Canada
092014   008478FRS15

SCOOBY-DOO!

THE FRIGHT AT ZOMBIE FARM

written by
Laurie S. Sutton

illustrated by
Scott Neely

THE MYSTERY INC. GANG!

SCOOBY-DOO

SKILLS: Loyal; super snout
BIO: This happy-go-lucky hound avoids scary situations at all costs, but he'll do anything for a Scooby Snack!

SHAGGY ROGERS

SKILLS: Lucky; healthy appetite
BIO: This laid-back dude would rather look for grub than search for clues, but he usually finds both!

FRED JONES, JR.

SKILLS: Athletic; charming
BIO: The leader and oldest member of the gang. He's a good sport—and good at them, too!

DAPHNE BLAKE

SKILLS: Brains; beauty
BIO: As a sixteen-year-old fashion queen, Daphne solves her mysteries in style.

VELMA DINKLEY

SKILLS: Clever; highly intelligent
BIO: Although she's the youngest member of Mystery Inc., Velma's an old pro at catching crooks.

← YOU CHOOSE →

SCOOBY-DOO!

A famous painter has disappeared, and now zombies run wild on his farm! Only YOU can help the Mystery Inc. gang solve this case of zombies on the loose.

Follow the directions at the bottom of each page. The choices YOU make will change the outcome of the story. After you finish one path, go back and read the others for more Scooby-Doo adventures!

YOU CHOOSE the path to solve the mystery of...

THE FRIGHT AT ZOMBIE FARM

The crime-solving kids of Mystery Incorporated drive down a twisting country road, but they aren't on a case. They've been invited to a weekend at a famous farmhouse.

"It sure was nice of our friend David Bush to ask us to come out to Bushytail Farm," Daphne says. "He's thinking of turning it into a quaint hotel."

"I can't wait to see the real Bushytail Farm. David has painted so many pictures of it, I feel like I already know the place," Velma says as she looks at an art book about the landscape paintings of Bushytail Farm.

Turn the page.

"You could say he's made a cottage industry out of it," Fred jokes as he drives the Mystery Machine.

The van passes a country fair. Delicious aromas float in the air. Suddenly Scooby-Doo and Shaggy pop up from the back of the Mystery Machine!

"Whoa! Like, I smell corn dogs!" Shaggy says and smacks his lips.

"Rand pie!" Scooby slobbers.

"How about some Scooby Snacks instead? We're almost at the farm," Daphne says as she shakes a box of the savory treats.

"Rokay!" Scooby and Shaggy say as Daphne tosses a couple of treats toward the pals. *CHOMP!* The two chowhounds gobble down the Scooby Snacks.

"Look! There's the entrance to Bushytail Farm. Just like in the paintings," Velma says. She points to a gate made of stone and iron.

Fred turns the Mystery Machine down the road leading to the gate. The pavement changes from smooth to rough. The van passes the old iron gates covered in rust and moss.

"Wait. This doesn't look like the paintings," Velma says, disappointed. "It looks . . . grungy. Are you on the right road, Fred?"

"I'm following the directions David gave me," Fred replies.

"Rit rooks haunted," Scooby shivers.

"Like, maybe we should go to the fair instead," Shaggy suggests. A picture of pies and cakes appears before his eyes.

"Too late. We're here," Fred announces.

The Mystery Machine stops in front of a farmhouse that looks like a sneeze could make it collapse.

The Mystery Inc. gang climbs out of the van. The quaint cottage in the famous paintings is really a dirty dump!

Turn the page.

"That's not how David painted it," Velma moans.

"Maybe he was using his artistic imagination," Daphne decides. "It sure isn't how I imagined it."

"Like, the place is a wreck!" Shaggy blurts. Scooby-Doo whimpers in agreement.

"Rit really rooks haunted," Scoobs says and hugs his pal Shaggy.

WHAM! The gang jumps when something hits the side of the Mystery Machine.

"Go away!" an old man shouts at them. His fist makes a dent in the side of the van.

"But we were invited!" Daphne protests.

"David Bush asked us to come here," Velma adds. "Where is he?"

"Don't know. I'm just the caretaker. Nobody tells me anything," the creepy old man replies. He turns and shuffles toward the barn. The gang is so rattled that no one notices him talking into a small microphone.

"Like, what are we going to do now?" Shaggy asks his friends.

"I have a plan!" Fred announces. "Let's split up and find David. He'll explain everything."

"He has a lot of explaining to do," Velma states as she grimaces at the sad image of her fantasy farmhouse. "Something is seriously wrong with this picture."

"Velma and I will look for David in the house," Daphne says.

"I'll search the barn," Fred volunteers.

"He might be at the fair. Scoobs and I will look there," Shaggy says as his stomach growls.

To follow Shaggy & Scooby, turn to page 12.
To follow Daphne & Velma, turn to page 14.
To follow Fred, turn to page 16.

Shaggy and Scooby-Doo leave the rest of Mystery Inc. at Bushytail Farm and walk to the fairgrounds to look for their friend, David. There are tents with food and games, a livestock pavilion, and plenty of rides. The two pals head straight for the fair food.

"Like, we need to keep up our strength," Shaggy explains as he fills his arms — and mouth — with food.

"Ri feel stronger ralready," Scooby agrees.

The buddies stroll through the fair. Their search for David is very casual. There is so much to distract them!

"Hey! Blueberry pies! I haven't had one of those in a long time!" Shaggy says and heads toward the pie stand.

"Rou had one resterday," Scooby reminds him.

"Sure, but it was a whole twenty-four hours ago. That's a long time!" Shaggy replies.

Full of baked goodies, Shaggy and Scooby wander toward the carnival rides. A roller coaster rises high above the fairgrounds.

"Hey, Scoob, maybe we can spot David from up there," Shaggy suggests and points to the top of the roller coaster.

"Rat's scary," Scooby whimpers.

"It's the highest point around here," Shaggy says. "Besides, it'll be fun."

"R-rokay, if rou say so," Scooby stammers.

Scooby follows Shaggy with knocking knees and chattering teeth. As they pass a tent, a finger pokes out from the flaps. It makes a beckoning gesture at Scooby-Doo.

"*Pssst!*" a voice hisses.

"Rhoo, me?" Scooby-Doo asks. He looks around to see if the voice is speaking to someone else.

"Yes, you," the voice replies. "Come here . . ."

If Scooby talks to the hand, turn to page 18.
If Scooby sticks with Shaggy, turn to page 25.

The gang splits up and goes in different directions. Daphne and Velma walk up to the farmhouse. The front porch is rickety and creaks when they step on it.

"Jeepers, this doesn't sound safe," Daphne observes.

"If it's this run down on the outside, I wonder how bad it is on the inside," Velma wonders. She grabs the door handle and turns the rusty metal knob.

The door swings open on old, noisy hinges. **CREEEEAK!** The only thing that Daphne and Velma can see inside is darkness. Velma starts to take a step over the threshold. Suddenly Daphne stops her!

"Wait!" Daphne warns. She reaches into her purse and pulls out a flashlight. "We're going to need this."

Daphne directs the bright beam around the gloomy room. All the furniture is covered with white sheets. The pale shapes look like huddled ghosts.

"Hello? David, are you here?" Daphne calls out. Silence is the only answer she gets.

"I don't think anyone has been here for a long time," Velma says. "Why were we invited to an abandoned farmhouse? There's a mystery here."

THUMP! The sound of something heavy rattles the floor under their feet.

"Jeepers! That sounded like it came from upstairs," Daphne gulps.

"No, I think it came from the basement," Velma says. "We better investigate both."

"You mean, split up?" Daphne asks. "But I always thought there was safety in numbers."

Daphne gives Velma an extra flashlight from her purse, and the two friends split up.

To follow Daphne upstairs, turn to page 21.
To Velma to the basement, turn to page 27.

The gang splits up to investigate the mystery of their missing friend. Fred decides to look in the barn. He walks toward the structure and eyes it suspiciously. It doesn't look anything like the David Bush paintings that made it famous. The red paint is peeling, and the shutters are crooked on their hinges. Shingles are missing on the roof, and the silo leans like the Tower of Pisa.

"Scooby's right. This place looks haunted," Fred says. "Maybe this is a job for Mystery Inc. after all."

Fred pulls on one of the big barn doors to go inside. It doesn't budge. Then he notices the padlock on the latch. The metal is rusted.

"I guess I'll have to find another way in," Fred decides.

Fred walks around the barn until he discovers a loose shutter. He pulls it off the barn window. Fred peers through the grimy glass but can't see much of anything. He rubs the surface with his hand. Suddenly Fred sees a shape move inside the barn.

"David! Is that you?" Fred shouts. The figure does not answer.

Fred is surprised to discover that the window isn't locked. He opens it and crawls through the opening.

"It's as quiet as a tomb in here," Fred says with a shudder. "And as dark as one, too. I wish I had a flashlight."

Suddenly a lantern flares to life in front of Fred's eyes. It illuminates a fearsome face!

"*Yaaa!*" Fred shouts in alarm. "A monster!"

If Fred runs up into the hayloft, turn to page 23.
If Fred jumps out the window, turn to page 29.

"You can talk to the hand," the voice whispers.

"What's going on, buddy?" Shaggy asks as he walks back to Scooby-Doo. "Did you find a clue?"

Suddenly the hand withdraws behind the tent flap.

"Rit's the rand," Scooby replies. He points to the tent. There is a giant palm painted on the canvas.

"Cool! Like, it's a fortune-teller!" Shaggy says. "Let's check it out. Maybe she can tell us where David is."

Shaggy opens the tent flap and goes inside before Scooby-Doo can blink twice.

Scooby feels more nervous about being left outside the tent than he does about being inside the tent. He spins all four legs and races through the flaps to follow Shaggy.

It's very dark inside the tent. Scooby can't see anything. Suddenly he bumps into something!

"*Yaaa!*" something yells.

"*Yaaa!*" Scooby shrieks.

SSSIIIZZZTT! A match is struck, and its
flame lights a candle. Shaggy and Scooby see
an old woman sitting at a round table in the
middle of the tent. A clear crystal ball reflects the
candle's weak glow.

"I have something to tell you," the old
woman says. She leans forward and the candle
flame makes her wrinkled face look like a
Halloween mask. "You have a choice. Go back to
the farm and find your friend, or stay here and
meet your doom!"

If Shaggy and Scooby decide to head back to the farm,
turn to page 32.

If Shaggy and Scooby decide to stay at the fair,
turn to page 48.

Daphne heads up the stairs. The second floor of the farmhouse is just as deserted as the first floor. Still, something has made a very large noise. Daphne hopes it's not a very large something!

"David, was that you?" Daphne asks loudly.

WHUMP! THUMP! The ceiling above Daphne's head sheds plaster dust. The broken light fixture shakes.

"Okay, there's definitely something in the attic," Daphne decides. "It's time to end this game of hide-and-seek."

Daphne's hand tightens around the flashlight as she starts to climb the narrow stairs to the attic.

Daphne has one foot on the bottom step when she feels a hand clamp down on her shoulder. She jumps in alarm.

"Jeepers!" Daphne shouts. "Velma, I thought you were going to investigate . . . the . . . basement . . . ?"

Turn the page.

Daphne's voice sticks in her throat as she turns around, expecting to see Velma. Instead she sees a looming gray shape with withered skin and glowing red eyes. It looks like a corpse. It reaches for her.

"*Yaaa!* A zombie!" Daphne yells.

She tries to run but her legs pinwheel in the air. The monster holds her by the collar and lifts her off the ground. Daphne twists around in a desperate attempt to escape. The ghoul's hand comes off! Daphne drops to the ground and runs!

If Daphne runs downstairs, turn to page 34.

If Daphne runs up to the attic, turn to page 52.

Fred is so startled by the frightening face that he doesn't think; he runs! His feet move so fast that they spin in place and kick up the loose straw. Fred leaves a cloud of dust behind him as he races through the barn.

BONK! Fred bounces off a stall door. **BAM!** He knocks into a stack of old crates. **BING! BANG!** Fred rebounds off everything in the barn like a pinball in a game.

Suddenly Fred sees a ladder. He climbs it up to the hayloft and dives behind a stack of stale hay bales. Fred shivers in fright, but he peeks over the bales. He wants to see what sort of monster Mystery Inc. has to face this time!

Fred peers down from the hayloft and looks around the barn. He is surprised to see that it's empty.

"Where did that monster go?" Fred wonders. "Did I imagine it?"

TAP! TAP! Something pokes Fred on the shoulder. He turns and sees the same ghoulish face.

Turn the page.

"Nope! I didn't imagine it!" Fred gulps.

"Why are you in here?" a rough voice demands.

A bright lantern is pushed close to Fred's face. He can barely see past the intense light, but he recognizes the caretaker.

"I'm searching for David Bush," Fred replies.

"He's not here. Leave!" the old man grumbles, then turns and is gone like a ghost.

"Where'd he go? How did he do that?" Fred gasps. "There's a mystery here, and I'm going to solve it!"

If Fred sees a mysterious light, turn to page 36.

If Fred follows a trail of footprints, turn to page 55.

Scooby-Doo stares at the creepy hand poking out of the tent flap. It looks weird. **SNIFF! SNIFF!** It smells weird.

"No ray!" Scooby decides. He runs and catches up to Shaggy.

"I got tickets to the roller coaster," Shaggy says. "We can see all of the fairgrounds from up there. Maybe we'll spot David."

The pals climb aboard the ride and the cars start the clattering journey to the first summit. Shaggy and Scooby are so busy looking around for David that they don't pay attention to the passengers in the cars behind them.

TAP! TAP! Something pokes Shaggy and Scooby on their shoulders. The pals turn around and see something more terrifying than the first plunge down the roller coaster tracks!

"*Yaaaa!*" they yell, and it's not because of the ride.

Turn the page.

"Zombies!" Shaggy shrieks.

The creatures make a grab at Scooby and Shaggy as the roller coaster banks into a sharp turn. The zombies miss! Their skeletal arms grasp thin air. The pals try to escape the ride, but the lap bars are locked tight.

The roller coaster screeches through a double loop and streaks down a second hill. The cars speed through a tunnel with flashing lights. The pals come out with their eyes spinning and seeing stars. So do the zombies.

At last the roller coaster splashes into an artificial lake. Water sprays up and soaks the riders. Shaggy and Scooby shake off the water. The zombies just moan in misery.

"That was refreshing!" Shaggy exclaims. "Now let's get out of here, Scoobs!"

"Which ray?" Scooby asks.

If Shaggy and Scooby run into the fine arts building, turn to page 68.

If Shaggy and Scooby run into the House of Mirrors, turn to page 86.

While Daphne investigates upstairs, Velma decides to explore downstairs. She holds the extra flashlight in her hand and tries to keep it from shaking. The house is very spooky. It's not like David's famous paintings at all!

Velma creeps cautiously through the living room to the kitchen. The curtains are closed on all the windows and the room is very dark. Suddenly Velma feels something brush her neck! The curtains move as if stroked by an invisible hand. She jumps in surprise.

"Jinkies!" Velma shouts. Then she notices that the basement door is open. "Oh, it's just a draft from the cellar."

Velma goes to the door and peers down the dark stairs.

"Hello? Is anyone down there?" Velma calls down the stairs. She hears no human reply.

Turn the page.

CLANK! Suddenly there is the sound of metal hitting metal. Velma follows the noise down into the cellar. Velma thinks she hears whispering. She swings the flashlight beam around the room. The light illuminates stacks of cardboard boxes and plenty of spider webs. Everything is covered with dust — except for an old wardrobe cabinet.

"Why is that piece of furniture so clean?" Velma wonders. "There's a mystery here."

Curious, Velma reaches for the handle. Before she can open the door of the wardrobe, it swings open all by itself! A ghoulish face stares out at her.

If Velma runs upstairs, turn to page 71.

If Velma gets trapped in the basement, turn to page 89.

A scowling face glares at Fred. The lantern's harsh light casts sharp shadows on the frowning forehead and snarling mouth.

Fred is so surprised that he jumps back out of the barn window. Something grabs his shirt and tries to keep him from escaping, but Fred tears free and runs as fast as his spinning legs can carry him.

"B-bushytail Farm is h-haunted," Fred stammers as he hides behind an old tractor. "I've got to tell the rest of the gang."

Fred turns around to head for the farmhouse but stops in his tracks. A group of ghouls stands in his path! They are as thin as skeletons. Their skin is as gray and wrinkled as an old elephant, and their hair hangs in patches from scabby scalps. The creatures reach for Fred with grasping fingers.

"*Yaaaa!* Zombies!" Fred yells.

Fred runs away from the zombies! Unfortunately he runs in the opposite direction from the farmhouse.

Turn the page.

The menacing monsters shuffle after Fred. Their legs are stiff and their limbs are creaky. They do not move very fast. As Fred flees across the farmyard he takes a chance and glances behind him. He sees the stumbling zombies struggling to chase him at turtle speed. Suddenly Fred does not feel so afraid.

"It looks like I have those zombies beat in the fifty-yard dash," Fred concludes. "I can circle around them and find Daphne and Velma in the farmhouse."

Fred is ready to sprint to his goal when he hears a roaring sound. He freezes as he sees a startling sight.

"As Scooby-Doo would say — ruh-roh!" Fred gulps.

If a haunted Mystery Machine chases Fred, turn to page 73.
If zombies drive the tractor and chase Fred, turn to page 92.

Shaggy and Scooby-Doo leave the fortune-teller's tent.

"Rikes!" Scooby says with a shiver.

"Like, I need a snack to calm my nerves," Shaggy declares.

"**SNIFF, SNIFF!** Rwaffles," Scooby announces and poses like a hunting dog pointing to its target.

"**SNIFF, SNIFF!** And I smell blueberry syrup," Shaggy says as he strikes the same stance. "Two noses are better than one, eh, Scoobs?"

The two pals race to the source of the delicious aromas. They load up on stacks of waffles with all the fixings. They can barely see where they're going as they balance the towers of food.

"Like, this should last us until we get back to the farm," Shaggy says.

CHOMP! CHOMP! GULP! The pals gobble up the waffles like two vacuum cleaners.

"Oops, I might have miscalculated," Shaggy shrugs. He is still hungry.

"Hee hee. Re, too," Scooby giggles as he slurps the syrup from his snout.

"I think we need a refill," Shaggy decides. "Like, we can head back to Bushytail Farm later."

"Rokay," Shaggy agrees as his tongue wags hungrily.

"You must leave now!" the old fortune-teller screeches as she suddenly blocks their path.

"Zoinks!" Shaggy yelps in surprise and leaps into Scooby's arms.

"Go away!" the woman warns.

"Funny, that creepy caretaker at the farm said the same thing," Shaggy says as the fortune-teller walks away. "Scoobs, I think I smell a mystery!"

"Ruh-roh" Scooby whimpers.

Turn to page 38.

Daphne wriggles loose from the grisly ghoul and runs down the stairwell. The passageway is very narrow, and she bumps her shoulders against the walls. The flashlight is jarred and almost falls out of her hands.

Daphne reaches the bottom of the attic stairs and risks taking a glance back at the zombie. It lumbers down the steps in plodding pursuit. Its stiff legs force the creature to go down the stairs one by one.

"It's time I took the express," Daphne decides. She leaps up onto the stair rail leading down to the living room.

Daphne slides down the railing like a surfer riding a wave. She speeds along the banister faster and faster. Suddenly she sees the post at the bottom.

"Uh-oh! End of the line," Daphne gasps.

Daphne reaches the end of the stair rail and dives off the banister. She sails over the post like a bird in flight.

Using her gymnastic skills, Daphne tucks her body into a ball and somersaults in the air. Then she thrusts out her legs for a landing.

SPROING! Daphne hits the couch cushions and bounces back into the air! The sheet covering the couch flies up, too. Daphne spreads out her arms and performs a perfect swan dive. Then she twists her body in midair and lands on her feet.

"I knew I could stick the landing!" Daphne says.

The sheet gently flutters down and lands on top of her just as the zombie thumps into the room. It looks around for its prey, but Daphne is hidden under the sheet.

Turn to page 42.

"It's the second time that guy has told Mystery Inc. to leave Bushytail Farm. And that's exactly why I think we should stay," Fred decides.

Fred starts to climb down the ladder but stops when he sees a sliver of light. It is shining between the old, cracked barn boards.

"I wonder where that's coming from," Fred mutters. "There's nothing on the other side of that wall except . . ."

Suddenly a trio of ghouls lunges out of a hidden door in the barn wall.

". . . zombies?!" Fred gasps.

Fred jumps backward to avoid their ghastly grip. He forgets he's on the ladder and falls!

Fred grabs a rung of the ladder and stops his tumble. The zombies snatch at him from the hayloft.

"Wh-where did they come from?" Fred stammers.

The creepy creatures snag Fred's wrist and start to pull him toward them.

"No way, zombay!" Fred rhymes as he twists out of their gruesome grasp. He snags a nearby rope and swings like a monkey. "Just call me Tarzan of the *oooofff*!"

Fred's triumphant cheer is cut short as he slams into a barn beam. He slides down to the ground and crumples into a limp heap. The zombies scurry down from the hayloft and stand over Fred like waiting vultures.

Turn to page 45.

"Follow that fortune-teller!" Shaggy says.

Scooby and Shaggy sneak after the old woman. She goes into a large tent and the pals peek inside. They immediately regret it. Gnarly hands grab them! A crowd of creepy creatures surrounds the two buddies.

"Zoinks! Zombies!" Shaggy gulps as the grinning ghouls close in.

"Run!" Scooby shrieks.

Shaggy and Scooby put their legs in reverse and speed backward out of the tent. The zombies rush in pursuit of the pals.

As soon as the people at the fair see the ghouls, everyone screams and starts to run. Tents are trampled. Food flies. Shaggy and Scooby catch the soaring snacks and shovel them into their mouths.

"Rummy!" Scooby burps.

"That gives me an idea," Shaggy says. He eyes a stack of pies in his hand.

"Hey, Scoobs! Let's play a game!" Shaggy shouts. "Knock over a zombie and win a prize."

Shaggy throws a pie at one of the ghouls. It hits the creature in the face and the monster falls to the ground. Shaggy pumps his fist in triumph. Seeing Shaggy's success, Scooby uses all four paws to toss fair food at the marauding monsters. **SMACK! SMACK! SMACK!** Zombies fall like bowling pins.

"Rahoo! Rike!" Scooby cheers. Suddenly he sees a swarm of ghastly ghouls heading in his direction. "Ruh-roh!"

"Look out *beloooow*!" Shaggy warns as he swings down a zip line and bombards the zombies with food and stuffed animals. Scooby scampers away as the creatures get buried.

Turn the page.

"You meddling kids! I told you to leave! Now you've ruined my perfect plan," the fortune-teller shouts as she stands next to the mound of motionless zombies.

"**SNIFF, SNIFF!** Hey! Rake!" Scooby-Doo says as he puts his scent-sensitive nose in the heap. He chomps down and comes up with a mask in his mouth.

"The fake zombies were supposed to scare people away from the fair and the farm," the fortune-teller confesses. "My brother is the farm's caretaker. We wanted the land on both properties so we could build a housing development."

"Shaggy! Scooby! We found David back at the farm!" Fred shouts as he and the rest of the Mystery Inc. gang arrive. "But you solved the mystery!"

"And your reward is all the corn dogs you can eat!" David declares.

THE END

To follow another path, turn to page II.

Daphne stands perfectly still as the zombie shuffles around the room. She can see it though the thin fabric. Daphne is surprised when she watches the ghoul take out a cell phone and speak into it!

"Since when does a zombie use a cell phone?" Daphne wonders. Then she answers her own question. "When it's a fake!"

Suddenly Daphne is not so afraid of the big bad ghoul. She decides it is time to play a trick on the counterfeit creature.

"*WOOOO!*" Daphne moans and shakes the sheet covering her. It makes a sound like a bat flapping its wings.

The zombie stops in its tracks.

"Wh . . . what was that?" it stammers in fright.

"*WOOOO!*" Daphne moans again. "You trespass in my domain!"

The zombie turns around and sees the pale shape of the shivering sheet in the dark room.

Daphne turns on the flashlight and illuminates the cloth from underneath. She waves her arms and makes the fabric flap.

"*Yaaa!* This place is haunted!" the zombie screams. Its legs spin like a windmill as it tries to escape.

"Not so fast," Daphne declares as she trips the ghoul with her purse.

The creature crashes to the ground and a mask flies off his head!

"Just as I thought. You're not a zombie, you're a fake!" Daphne says.

"What's all the commotion?" Velma says as she runs up the stairs from the basement. "I found David downstairs."

Turn the page.

"What's going on here?" Fred asks as he runs into the house from the barn.

"That's what I'm about to find out," Daphne says. She ties up the fake zombie with the sheet.

"You meddling kids!" the man grumbles. "I wanted to turn Bushytail Farm into a tourist attraction, but David wouldn't let me."

"Cousin James!" David gasps.

"So, in revenge, you scared people away with your zombie disguise to ruin the farm's reputation," Daphne concludes.

"And I would have gotten away with it, too," the man mutters.

"Another case solved by Mystery Inc.!" Fred declares.

THE END

To follow another path, turn to page 11.

"Ooooh, what hit me?" Fred wonders as he slowly wakes up. He looks around and sees that he is tied to a chair inside a laboratory.

"Welcome back to the land of the living," the old caretaker says. The trio of zombies stands behind him.

"Wow! I can't believe you hid all this on Bushytail Farm!" Fred exclaims.

"What? How do you know that?" the caretaker says.

"I figure you couldn't have taken me too far from the barn," Fred replies. "We're either under the farmhouse or . . ."

"We're in the silo!" the man snaps. "And you should have left when I told you to!"

"Not a chance! Where there's a mystery, there's Mystery Inc.!" Fred proclaims.

Turn the page.

"Mystery Inc. is nothing but a bunch of troublesome teenagers," the caretaker says. "I didn't think much about it when my cousin David invited you here."

"Okay, now I get it. You're an angry relative looking for revenge . . . or maybe a gold mine or an inheritance. I lose track sometimes," Fred says as he secretly tries to untie the ropes that bind him to the chair.

"None of the above," the old man declares. He reaches up to his scalp, grabs a fistful of hair, and yanks off a mask. The zombies behind him do the same.

"*Awww!* Why did you do that?" Fred complains. "I could have figured it out for myself. I hate spoilers!"

Fred leaps into action! He breaks free and tackles the fake caretaker. The false zombies are knocked down, too. As quick as a rodeo star, Fred ties up the imposters with the rope.

"You meddling kid! My experiment is ruined," the unmasked man groans. "I built this secret lab to create a special popcorn from Bushytail Farm corn. The patent is worth millions!"

"Why not work with your cousin David?" Fred asks.

"He's a painter, not a scientist," the man grumbles.

"So you found some lab techs to help you," Fred concludes. He looks at the other three prisoners. "I bet dressing up as zombies wasn't in the job description."

The men shake their heads.

"Another mystery is solved!" Fred cheers. "Now, is there a sample of that popcorn? I'm sure Scooby-Doo will love it!"

THE END

To follow another path, turn to page 11.

Suddenly the candle goes out and the fortune-teller's tent becomes as dark as night.

"Well, here we are, left in the dark. Again." Shaggy sighs.

"Ret's ro," Scooby whimpers.

The two pals grope around and finally find their way out of the tent. Outside, things are not much brighter. Gloomy storm clouds gather over the fairgrounds.

"It's as dark out here as it was in there," Shaggy observes.

"Ruh-roh, it rooks like rain," Scooby warns.

CRAAAACK-A-BOOOOM! A loud clap of thunder explodes on top of them. The shock wave nearly knocks the friends off their feet. Sheets of rain start to fall.

"Like, we've got to get out of this storm!" Shaggy says.

Shaggy and Scooby turn around to run back into the fortune-teller's tent, but it isn't there anymore!

The fortune-teller's tent has disappeared mysteriously, so Shaggy and Scooby run inside the nearby livestock pavilion. They are shocked at what they see. All of the livestock is as gray as old ashes. Their eyes are vacant and staring. The cows don't moo, they moan.

"These critters look like, like . . ." Shaggy starts to say.

"Zombies!" Scooby finishes for him and points his paw.

A crowd of creepy creatures staggers toward Shaggy and Scooby and surround the two pals. Shaggy and Scooby-Doo hug each other and tremble in fright.

"We're doomed! The fortune-teller was right!" Shaggy wails.

"I knew you boys wouldn't listen to me," a voice says. Shaggy and Scooby blink in surprise when they see the fortune-teller standing behind the ghouls. "I hate being right."

Turn the page.

The old woman tosses her crystal ball at the zombies. It shoots out thick black smoke. Shaggy and Scooby are engulfed in the cloud. So are the zombies.

"Run!" the fortune-teller shouts at the pals.

Shaggy and Scooby race toward the glowing red exit sign in the dense smoke. They burst through the doors and out into the rain. The fortune-teller is waiting for them.

"It's not over yet," she warns them as zombies pour out of the pavilion.

"Like, who are you?" Shaggy asks.

"You're Mystery Inc. — figure it out," the old lady grins. "But first, we've got to get away from these gruesome ghouls."

Turn to page 58.

Daphne escapes the zombie by running up another set of stairs to the attic. She hopes there is a door with a lock! The staircase is narrow and steep. Daphne bumps her shoulders against the walls with almost every step. The flashlight is jostled and nearly falls out of her hand. Finally Daphne reaches the top of the stairs.

"Thank goodness the attic has a door! I can hide in there!" Daphne sighs with relief.

Daphne turns the antique knob, but the door won't open. She jiggles and twists the handle.

"Oh, no! It's locked! And I don't have the key!" Daphne moans.

A gurgling moan rises up from the bottom of the stairs. Daphne hears the sound of heavy feet on the stair treads. *THUMP! THUMP! THUMP!* The zombie lumbers closer and closer.

The creature shambles slowly up the stairs toward Daphne. The locked door stands between her and safety.

"There's got to be something in my purse that I can use to open this door," Daphne mumbles to herself as she stirs her hand around inside the bag.

"This might work," Daphne decides and holds up a ballpoint pen in the flashlight beam.

Trying to ignore the thumping sound of zombie footsteps coming up the stairs, Daphne pokes the pen into the door lock. Daphne wiggles the pen around until she hears a click. She grabs the knob and opens the door just in time!

Turn the page.

Daphne runs through the door and into the attic. She slams the door behind her and leans her body against it. The zombie pounds on the door with his fists.

"That was close!" Daphne gasps as she bolts the door behind her. "But I'm not out of trouble yet."

Daphne swings the flashlight beam around the attic. The room is dark and full of strange shapes. She hopes the shapes are just draped sheets like downstairs. Suddenly the beam illuminates more zombies!

"*Yaaa!*" Daphne shouts and jumps in surprise.

But the creatures do not move. They hang like limp socks on the wall of the attic. Daphne pokes one with her ballpoint pen. It collapses to the floor and lies still.

Turn to page 62.

Fred climbs down from the hayloft. The old caretaker scared him at first, but now Fred is curious.

"That guy is trying very hard to get me to leave. That's why I'm going to stay," Fred decides.

Fred looks around the barn for clues. He spots some footprints going into a stall. Fred follows the trail until it ends against the back wall of the enclosure.

"That's weird. The footprints vanish into thin air, just like the old man," Fred observes. "I'll bet there's a secret passage!"

Fred runs his hands over the old barn boards, looking for a hidden latch. All he gets is splinters. Suddenly Fred trips on something in the straw. He falls face-first and makes a surprising discovery!

Fred sprawls in the straw, but he has solved the mystery of the vanishing footprints.

"There's a latch to a trap door," Fred gasps. "The secret door is in the floor!"

Turn the page.

He gets to his feet and grabs the latch handle. Fred pulls open the hatch. He can just make out the shape of a ladder leading down into the gloom. Fred leans over for a closer look. Suddenly a pair of eyeballs blinks back at him!

"*Yaaa!*" Fred shouts in alarm. He tries to back away from the trap door but slips on the loose straw. It's like ice under his feet and he slips and falls right into the hole!

THUMP! Fred crashes into a large body in the dark. Even though Fred can't see anything, he knows that whatever it is, it isn't human! His face is covered with its slobbery drool.

"Fred! Are we ever glad to see you!" Shaggy cries and hugs his friend.

"Reah! Re too!" Scooby-Doo whimpers and wraps his paws around Shaggy and Fred.

"Shaggy? Scooby? What are you guys doing down here?" Fred asks, surprised. What he thought was a monster in the dark turns out to be his two pals.

"Like, we sort of got lost on the way to the fairgrounds," Shaggy admits. "There are all sorts of creepy tunnels down here."

"You found a clue to the mystery of the missing caretaker," Fred says.

"We did? How about that, Scoobs?" Shaggy laughs. "We did something right!"

Turn to page 65.

Shaggy, Scooby, and the fortune-teller take off toward the nearest game tent. Inside, they hide among the stuffed toy prizes. Shaggy disguises himself as a giant panda bear. Scooby puts a pair of fuzzy rabbit ears on his head and pretends to be a bunny. The fortune-teller grabs a plush unicorn and holds it up in front of her face.

"This isn't camouflage, this is crazy!" the old lady complains.

"Hee-hee!" Scooby chuckles.

"Zoinks! The zombies are coming!" Shaggy yells.

The ghouls spread out to look for their prey. Some of them hobble up to the game tent. They pick up the game balls and start throwing them at the targets. The zombies have terrible aim. The balls hit the stuffed toys instead of the targets!

"*OW! OW!*" Shaggy yelps as the balls knock off his panda disguise.

"Ruh-roh!" Scooby gulps.

The zombies swarm all over Shaggy and Scooby-Doo like ants on a cupcake. The pals try to run but are weighed down by the gruesome ghouls. There is no escape!

"You meddling American kids!" a voice declares with a strange accent. "You have interrupted my experiment."

Shaggy and Scooby poke their heads out from the pile of zombies. They see a figure wearing a dark cloak and a black hat. The brim of the hat hides the person's face in shadow.

"Like, we're sorry. We were just looking for our friend," Shaggy explains.

"Well, you found trouble!" the figure snaps. He holds a spray can in front of their noses. "This special gas will make you into mindless drones, and you will obey my every command!"

"Oh, I get it! These aren't zombies, they're test subjects," Shaggy realizes.

"Correct! And you will become one of them!" the figure says.

Turn the page.

"Not so fast, Dr. X!" the fortune-teller commands as she leaps out from under the toys.

The old woman throws a small crystal ball at the can and knocks it to the ground. The container shoots a jet of gas into the figure's hidden face! The mysterious stranger turns zombie-gray and collapses to the ground.

"Thanks for helping me capture the rogue scientist, Dr. X," the fortune-teller says as she removes her old-lady mask to reveal a young face. "I'm Agent Michelle Barr."

"Scoobs and I are glad to help. Like, what did we do?" Shaggy replies.

"You made Dr. X come out of hiding so I could catch him in the act," Agent Barr explains. "You guys are very skilled."

Shaggy and Scooby slap a high five. "Scooby-Dooby-Doo!" they shout.

THE END

To follow another path, turn to page 11.

Daphne jumps backward in surprise as the boneless ghoul drops to the floor of the attic like a sack of grain. *WHOMP!*

"That isn't a zombie," Daphne realizes. "It's a clue to this mystery."

Suddenly the attic door bursts open with a crashing *BLAM!* There isn't just one zombie anymore. The creature that chased Daphne up the stairs has brought along some fearsome friends! The gruesome ghouls stretch out their arms toward Daphne.

"*Yaaa!*" Daphne shrieks and tries to run.

She doesn't get far. Daphne accidentally runs into an old painter's easel. Then she stumbles and bounces off a stack of stored paintings. The canvases scatter on the floor. Beautiful landscape paintings spread out all over the attic.

"*Ahhh!*" one of the zombies moans and kneels next to the paintings.

"*Miiiiine!*" another zombie hisses like a snake as it pushes the other zombie away.

"*Nooooo!*" a third zombie shrieks.

Daphne hides behind a dresser in a dark corner of the attic and watches the zombies as they fight over the paintings.

"That is not normal," Daphne realizes. "Since when are zombies art collectors?"

Concealed in the shadows, Daphne watches the gaunt ghouls battle each other for possession of the paintings.

"That's because they aren't zombies, they're fakes! They want David's paintings!" Daphne gasps.

Then she frowns with determination. "I don't think so!"

Daphne is determined to save her friend's paintings. She creeps over to the zombie that fell off the wall.

"This isn't a zombie, it's a costume!" Daphne discovers. "Two can play this game!"

Daphne puts the zombie mask over her head and zips up the creepy outfit.

Turn the page.

Daphne jumps out at the gang of thieves.

"*Wooooo!* I'm the ghost of Bushytail Farm!" Daphne shouts.

All the zombies pull off their masks and run! Only one of them stays. He can't let go of the paintings. The Mystery Inc. gang arrives just as Daphne pulls off the man's fake zombie face.

"Jeff Kelly! You wrote the art book about Bushytail Farm!" Velma says.

"I used fake zombies to scare everyone away so I could look for David's lost paintings," Jeff confesses. "The art could have been mine if it wasn't for you meddling kids!"

THE END

To follow another path, turn to page 11.

"I'm sure if we find the caretaker, we'll find our friend, David," Fred decides.

"Like, why don't we just ask those guys," Shaggy suggests and points to a trio of shadowy figures. But as soon as they step out of the gloom, Shaggy sees they aren't "guys" at all. "Uh-oh, they're zombies!"

"Run!" Fred yells.

The pals clamber over each other to climb up the ladder. **BOOM!** The trap door slams shut above their heads.

"Ruh-roh," Scooby gulps.

"We're doomed," Shaggy moans.

"Don't worry. We can outrun them. Zombies are slow," Fred says.

The creepy creatures rush toward the pals and grab them in a ghoulish grip.

"Well, they're slow in the movies," Fred groans.

"Like, now what?" Shaggy asks. "We need a plan!"

Turn the page.

"Sorry, guys, I'm fresh out," Fred sighs. "We're doomed."

The zombies march Fred, Shaggy, and Scooby through the dark tunnels.

"Wow, it's a maze down here," Fred observes. "No wonder you two got lost."

The pals are taken to an underground room filled with office furniture and computer equipment. Sitting behind a desk is the old caretaker. He jumps to his feet when he sees the Mystery Inc. gang.

"You idiots!" the man shouts at the zombies. "Why did you bring those meddling kids here?"

"Because that was my plan," Fred announces. "I wanted to get to the bottom of this mystery. I had no idea it would be fifty feet below ground."

Fred twists around and snatches the masks off two of the zombies. Once they are exposed as human, they run away. The caretaker is left without reinforcements.

The old man sits down in his chair, defeated.

"Now that you've discovered my headquarters, my plan is ruined," the caretaker grumbles. "I was going to use these tunnels for my smuggling operation."

"You used those fake zombies to frighten away visitors," Fred deduces. "Plus, you let Bushytail Farm get run down so no one would want to visit."

"Yes. And I would have gotten away with it if it hadn't been for you meddling Mystery Inc. kids," the man complains.

"So, like, where's our friend, David?" Shaggy wants to know.

"I sent him on a European art tour," the caretaker says. "He's been gone for months."

"Then who sent us the invitation to visit the farm?" Fred wonders.

"It wasn't me," the old man shrugs.

"Rit's another mystery!" Scooby says.

THE END

To follow another path, turn to page 11.

Shaggy and Scooby make a hasty retreat away from the roller coaster. They run through the deserted fairgrounds looking for the exit. Soon they lose all sense of direction.

"We've been going around in circles," Shaggy pants as the pals come to a halt.

"Re're lost!" Scooby moans.

Suddenly they see the ghouls shambling toward them.

"Zoinks! It's the zombies! They found us!" Shaggy shrieks.

"Re're doomed!" Scooby whimpers.

The pals run into the nearest tent, hoping to hide. They are surprised by what they find.

"David!" Shaggy shouts.

Their friend stands in front of a large painting of a landscape. He has brushes in his hand and stands next to a table filled with tubes of oil paint.

"Oh hi, guys! I'm just trying to fix this painting. I can't seem to get the lighting right," David says.

Shaggy and Scooby realize that they are in a fine arts building. David's paintings fill the tent.

"No wonder we couldn't see David from up on the roller coaster! He was inside this tent the whole time," Shaggy gasps as he smacks his forehead with the palm of his hand.

"Where's the rest of the gang?" David asks.

Suddenly the pack of zombies bursts into the tent. They surround Shaggy, Scooby, and David.

"That's not the gang," David gulps.

The creatures lunge at the friends. David grabs the big painting he is working on and smashes it down over the heads of the creatures.

Turn to page 75.

The frightful sight of a zombie in the wardrobe startles Velma, and she drops the flashlight. She can hear it hit the ground, but she can't see it. Everything around her is as dark as midnight.

"Jinkies! This is as bad as losing my glasses!" Velma moans as she gropes around the floor. Suddenly she feels something cold and clammy grab her ankle.

"*Yaaa!*" Velma yells and twists out of the zombie's ghoulish grip.

Desperately, Velma crawls toward a single spot of light — the basement door at the top of the stairs. As soon as her hands touch the wooden steps, Velma knows where she is. She climbs up the stairs on all fours like a monkey up a tree.

SLAM! Velma shuts the basement door behind her and leans her weight against it.

Turn the page.

Velma does not have time to catch her breath after her narrow escape. ***WHAM! WHAM!*** The basement door shudders behind her as the ghoul slams its fists against the wood.

"Why is there a zombie in the basement?" Velma gasps. "And how did it get up the stairs so fast? Zombies are supposed to be slow."

Velma decides to think about those questions later! She grabs a kitchen chair and wedges it under the doorknob.

"The chair-under-the-door trick always works in the movies. I hope it works in real life," Velma says. "But, just in case it doesn't, I need a plan."

Turn to page 79.

"The Mystery Machine! It started up all by itself!" Fred gasps. "How? It doesn't have a remote ignition button."

The lime-green van spins its wheels in the dirt and guns its engine. It sounds like the growl of a wild animal. The headlights blaze to life. They look like the glaring eyes of a predatory beast. The Mystery Machine lunges toward Fred.

"It's alive!" Fred yells. He turns and runs right at the zombies.

The clumsy creatures do not get out of the way in time. Fred barrels into them. So does the Mystery Machine. The zombies are tossed high into the air. They flap their stiff arms like birds, but they are more like flightless penguins than soaring swans. They drop back down and land on top of the van.

The zombies cling to the Mystery Machine with boney fingers as the van chases Fred around the farmyard. He can barely keep ahead of the mad machine.

Turn the page.

He jumps up on a fence and runs along the top to get out of the van's path, but the Mystery Machine slams into the side of the fence and makes Fred lose his balance. He falls into the pigpen and comes up covered in swine slime.

"*Eeeeww!*" Fred groans.

"Fred! What's going on?" Daphne shouts. She stands on the porch of the farmhouse with Velma and their friend, David. "We found David in the basement then heard all this noise!"

Suddenly the Mystery Machine pivots on its back tires and peels off toward the farmhouse.

"Jinkies!" Velma yells as she barely dodges the van.

"Jeepers!" Daphne gasps as she grabs David and jumps out of the way.

Turn to page 82.

"I didn't really like that painting anyway," David states as he, Shaggy, and Scooby flee.

The trio runs out the back of the exhibit tent and jumps into David's farm ATV. Shaggy grabs the wheel and puts the pedal to the metal. The cart zips away at a plodding ten miles an hour.

"Like, this isn't much faster than those zombies," Shaggy observes.

David shrugs. "There's no need for speed at Bushytail Farm."

The friends drive back to the farm. They are met by the creepy caretaker, which makes David angry.

"What are you still doing here? I fired you for not taking care of Bushytail while I was traveling," David growls. "You let the place become a ruin."

"You should have stayed away. All of you," the man grumbles. "Now I have to take drastic measures."

The old man speaks into a small microphone.

Turn the page.

A moment later zombies pour out of the house and the barn. Shaggy and Scooby are shocked to see that Fred, Daphne, and Velma are part of the gruesome group. They have been turned into gray-faced ghouls, too!

"Now it's your turn to follow my commands," the caretaker says as he dangles a hypnotic pendulum in front of Shaggy, Scooby, and David. Their eyes swirl in their sockets. Scooby-Doo blinks in confusion.

"Yes, master," Shaggy and David moan. "Your wish is our command."

"Follow me. I have a fortune to claim," the caretaker proclaims. He gestures and all the zombies shamble after him. Scooby-Doo stays.

"What?" the old man shouts. "My hypnotic power doesn't work on animals. That canny canine fooled me!"

Scooby-Doo jumps over the zombies and lands on top of the creepy caretaker.

The pendulum is knocked out of the caretaker's hands. Suddenly all the ghouls' faces turn back to healthy human faces. Shaggy, Fred, Daphne, and Velma get up and hug their pal.

"Scooby-Doo, you saved us!" Daphne says as she kisses the pooch on the snout.

"It's a good thing you're a hound and not a human," Velma laughs and hugs Scooby.

"You meddling kids! I turned people into zombies to be my workers in the gem mine that's under the farm and the fairgrounds," the man confesses.

"There's wealth under Bushytail Farm?" David exclaims. "Now I can afford to turn the farmhouse into a quaint hotel. Thanks, Mystery Incorporated!"

THE END

To follow another path, turn to page 11.

Velma looks around the deserted farmhouse kitchen for a way to defend herself against the zombie.

"Where's a frying pan or a rolling pin when I need one?" Velma wonders aloud as she searches through the cabinets and drawers. "Maybe it's time for Plan B!"

BWAM! BWAM! The basement door shudders on its hinges as the creature tries to break it down. **SMASH!** Suddenly the wood splinters. The cellar door bursts wide open. Instead of one zombie, now there are four gruesome ghouls!

"Get her!" they shout.

Velma is surrounded. The moldy monsters reach out to grab her.

"Jinkies! I'd better think of a Plan B — fast!" Velma gulps.

Velma backs into the pantry of the farmhouse kitchen. The shelves are full of canned food.

Turn to page 80.

"I think this stuff is older than you guys!" Velma chuckles as she tosses the cans at the zombies. *THUMP! THWAK! BONK!*

"*Owww! Owww!*" the zombies howl as they fall onto the kitchen floor.

"You're not zombies, you're fakes!" Velma proclaims. "I realized it when you chased me up the stairs. Real zombies don't run that fast."

"R-real zombies? Where?" the ghouls stammer as Velma stands over them. She puts her foot on the chest of one of them, leans over, and pulls off his mask. A human face is revealed.

"Who are you and what are you doing?" Velma demands. "Wait. Let me solve the mystery."

"The solution to this mystery is simple," she says "You're all David's relatives and want something on Bushytail Farm."

"Close enough," the unmasked man reveals. "We're his cousins, and we teamed up to find the buried treasure!"

"What buried treasure?" asks David Bush as he comes into the kitchen with the rest of the Mystery Inc. gang.

"There's a fortune in gold from a secret mine on the property. It's a family legend," one of the fake zombies says.

"That legend isn't real. I made it up for the Bushytail books!" David declares.

"Another myth busted, and another mystery solved," Velma concludes.

THE END

To follow another path, turn to page 11.

The van misses Daphne, Velma, and David and screeches to a halt. It revs its engine as if trying to decide who to chase next. The zombies slide off the roof of the van and collapse on the ground. They try to get to their feet, but they are too dizzy from the wild ride.

"*Yaaa!* Zombies!" Daphne shrieks. "Scooby was right! Bushytail Farm is haunted!"

Suddenly the Mystery Machine roars to life and spins its wheels. It gets a grip and takes off toward Fred! He slips and slides in the squishy mud but his feet just spin in one spot.

"I'm doomed!" Fred gulps.

"He's doomed!" his friends moan.

"Scooby-Dooby-Doo!" comes a triumphant yell.

"Yeah! Like, what he said!" echoes another voice.

Suddenly Scooby and Shaggy land on top of the Mystery Machine. They wrap a rope around the front bumper like reins on a mustang.

The pals pull up on the rope. The van stops inches away from Fred! It pants out puffs of exhaust from the tailpipe and then settles down to a gentle idle.

"There, there, big fella," Shaggy says as he pats the van on the roof as if calming a spooked horse. Fred, Daphne, Velma, and David join their pals next to the Mystery Machine.

"Wow! That was a great rodeo roundup!" Daphne says.

"But why did the Mystery Machine act like that?" Fred asks.

"I can solve that mystery. Look!" Velma declares. She points to an antenna attached to the van.

"That antenna was receiving remote control signals," Velma announces. "Someone used the Mystery Machine to scare us."

"Like, those zombies are scaring me and Scoobs just fine!" Shaggy whimpers.

Turn to page 85.

"Reah! I rate zombies," Scooby-Doo agrees.

"Don't worry, those aren't zombies," Velma declares. She pulls the mask off one of the ghouls. A pair of remote control glasses falls from his face.

"Chase Carson!" Fred gasps. "You're a champion mini-track race car driver."

"I invented a new remote control technology and wanted to build a factory for robot cars on this property, but that painter guy wouldn't sell it to me," Chase confesses and glares at David.

"So you hired fake zombies to scare people and devalue the farm," Daphne deduces.

"And I would have gotten away with it except for you meddling kids," Chase grumbles.

"Another mystery solved!" Shaggy says. He grabs the remote control to the Mystery Machine. "My turn to drive!"

VROOOOOMMMM!

THE END

To follow another path, turn to page 11.

Shaggy and Scooby jump out of the roller coaster car and sprint as fast as their legs can spin. The zombies struggle off the ride and stumble after the two pals. When the people at the fair see the ghastly ghouls they scream and run away! Suddenly Shaggy and Scooby are the only humans left at the fair. It's easy for the zombies to spot them.

"We can hide in here, pal!" Shaggy says as he grabs Scooby and pulls him into the House of Mirrors.

Distorted images of the teen and his dog stretch and shrink in the weird light inside the pavilion. The pals wave their hands and stick out their tongues at their silly reflections.

"Hey Scoobs, you're nine feet tall!" Shaggy laughs at his friend's extra-long shape.

"Hee-hee! Rou have two heads!" Scooby giggles.

Shaggy's eyes go wide in alarm as he looks in the fun-house mirror and sees that he has grown an extra head! It is gray and wrinkled and looks like a rotting raisin.

"*Yaaa!* I'm turning into a mutant zombie!" Shaggy yells. Suddenly a second pair of arms reaches around and clutches him. "*Yaaa!* Like, now I have four arms, too!"

"Rit's the zombies!" Scooby yelps and jumps into Shaggy's arms. Only one pair of limbs catches him.

"*Yaaa!*" the pals shout together as the creepy creatures surround them.

"Like, this fun house isn't fun anymore," Shaggy announces. "Let's get out of here!"

The pals burst through the circle of ghouls and run as fast as they can!

Shaggy and Scooby race out of the House of Mirrors. The fairgrounds are deserted. All the visitors have fled in fright. Shaggy and Scooby do the same!

The pals run toward the exit. They have safety in their sights when the delicious aroma of pastries reaches their noses. Their feet halt in their tracks. *SCREEECH! SNIFF! SNIFF!*

Turn the page.

Freedom is forgotten. The buddies get on all fours like bloodhounds and follow the scent. It takes them to a staggering sight.

"Like, how did we miss this?" Shaggy gasps as he gazes up at a giant tent that looks like a cupcake castle.

"Rit rooks rummy!" Scooby says. His mouth waters so much that it makes a pool of drool.

Shaggy looks to the left and right. He doesn't see any zombies chasing them.

"I suppose we could take a look inside," Shaggy decides.

Turn to page 96.

Velma is so surprised to see a zombie that she drops the flashlight. It hits the floor and goes out. She can't see anything, but neither can the zombie.

"If I keep very quiet, that creepy creature won't know where I am," Velma tells herself as she crawls across the floor. She can hear the zombie stumbling around in the blacked-out basement. "Too bad I don't know where I am, either!"

Velma strains her vision against the darkness. Even wearing her glasses she can't see a thing. Suddenly she spies a glimmer of light.

"I hope that's the door to the kitchen," Velma whispers as she makes her way toward the dim glow.

Velma crawls on her hands and knees toward the weak spot of light as fast as she can. In her hurry her knee hits the fallen flashlight. **CLICK!** Suddenly its bright beam spears the darkness. Velma finds herself face-to-face with the zombie! Both of them jump back in surprise.

Turn the page.

"*Yaaa!*" Velma yells.

"*Yaaa!*" the zombie shrieks. The creature is so startled that it stumbles backward into the wardrobe. It disappears down a hole with a lingering cry. "*Yaaaaaaa!*"

Velma picks up the flashlight and points it into the wardrobe. The zombie is gone!

"That's a very interesting vanishing act," Velma declares. "And as far as I know, zombies don't do magic. There's a mystery here!"

Velma peers into the wardrobe and looks around the interior with the flashlight. There is a hole in the bottom. The flashlight beam reaches only a few feet before it is eaten up by darkness.

"I've read *Alice in Wonderland,* and this looks like a very weird rabbit hole," Velma decides. "I also know a clue when I see one."

Velma jumps down the opening. **SWOOOOH!** She slides down a metal chute and lands in an underground room. She also lands on the unmoving body of the zombie!

"Jinkies!" Velma exclaims as she scrambles to get off the ghastly ghoul. "Yuck! Yuck! Wait a minute, something's weird about this guy."

Velma runs her fingers over the zombie's face. Her expression wrinkles up in disgust.

Turn to page 99.

The roar of a revved-up engine echoes across the farmyard. ***VROOOM! VROOOOM!*** Fred is astonished to see the zombies are all aboard the old tractor. One of the creatures grips the steering wheel. It grins at Fred like a cat staring at a mouse it's about to chase.

"Uh-oh. It looks like those slow pokes are about to put the pedal to the metal," Fred says.

The tractor wheels spin in the dirt as the zombie driver steps on the gas. The huge back tires spit grass and gravel out from under the wide treads. With so much traction in the back, the front wheels lift off the ground.

"I can't believe I'm seeing this! A zombie wheelie!" Fred exclaims.

"That gives new meaning to the expression 'popping a *monster* wheelie'," Fred observes as the zombies lean the tractor back on its rear tires.

SCREEEECH! The driver finds the gear and accelerates the vehicle toward Fred. The exhaust stack belches black soot.

Turn to page 94.

"Someone needs to check that carburetor," Fred comments as he coughs in the cloud of stinky smoke.

The tractor zooms at Fred. He performs his own version of a wheelie as his feet spin in place. Soil sprays out in a fantail behind him as he digs out a rut in the ground. Suddenly Fred is five feet deep! He can't jump out of the trench in time.

"I'm doomed!" Fred gasps.

Fred watches as the tractor races toward him. For such an old vehicle it has enormous power. It also has a terrible driver. The monster misses Fred completely! The tractor skids in a tight circle. All but one wheel comes off the ground and the machine spins like a ballet dancer. **_WHAAAAM!_** It does not land like one.

The tractor and the zombies lie flat on the ground. Fred sees his chance to escape! He scrambles out of the hole he dug himself into and runs toward the orchard.

He has a plan. He'll hide in the leafy trees and watch where the zombies go.

"I'll follow them and get to the bottom of this mystery," Fred decides as he climbs up into the branches.

Turn to page 103.

Shaggy and Scooby go inside the cupcake castle tent. They enter a pastry paradise. There are shelves filled with cakes and tarts and pies of every kind stacked up to the ceiling.

"Like, pinch me, I'm dreaming!" Shaggy sighs. "Ow!"

"Hee-hee!" Scooby chuckles as he quickly hides his paw behind his back.

"Hey, I recognize these cupcakes. They're Whammy Grammy Cupcakes," Shaggy says. He looks around the tent. He and Scooby are the only ones there. "Do you think it would be okay if we had a little taste? You know, like, samples?"

Shaggy reaches out and takes a cupcake. Before he knows it he has an armload.

"What are you doing here?" a voice demands.

"Zoinks!" Shaggy yelps and jumps in surprise as an old woman pops up from behind one of the shelves.

"Rit's a zombie!" Scooby wails.

Shaggy is so startled that the sweets in his grasp go flying into the air. Scooby gobbles them up before they hit the ground.

"I'm not a zombie, I'm just a little old lady," the woman says.

Scooby-Doo isn't convinced at first. He sniffs the woman, and she smells of cake and frosting.

"She smells rummy!" Scooby declares.

"It's not safe for you to be here," Shaggy warns the old woman. "There are zombies on the loose."

Suddenly a gang of ghouls rushes into the cupcake tent. Shaggy and Scooby shriek in fright, and their hair stands on end.

"Lady, look out!" Shaggy shouts.

"Oh, they won't hurt me," the old woman assures them. She cackles with hideous laughter. "They're my sons!"

Gruesome zombies surround Shaggy and Scooby. The old woman stands in the center like their queen.

Turn the page.

"Meet the real Whammy Grammy family," she announces. All of the zombies take off their masks revealing unfriendly faces.

"Like, I should have known," Shaggy moans.

"I want to expand my cupcake business and need land to build a new factory. Bushytail Farm and the fairgrounds are perfect properties," the woman explains.

"So your sons dressed up as zombies to scare people away and free up the properties," Shaggy realizes. The ghouls close in on the pals. "Wait! I have a last request. Scoobs and I want cupcakes as our last meal."

Before the woman can answer, Shaggy and Scooby become a tornado of food frenzy. They consume every crumb of cake, pie, and pastry.

"You ate all my inventory! I'm ruined!" the woman wails. "You meddling kids!"

"Sweet victory!" Shaggy burps.

THE END

To follow another path, turn to page 11.

Velma kneels over the motionless zombie. She notices something about the creature that attracts her analytical eye. Velma reaches out and touches the zombie's face.

"*Ewww!*" Velma groans. An oily slime drips from her fingers. "What is this gunk?"

Before Velma can think about that, more zombies surround her! They grab her and drag her down a tunnel. This time Velma doesn't try to escape. She's curious. There is a mystery under Bushytail Farm, and she is determined to solve it!

Velma is taken to a small room and shoved inside.

"Velma?" a voice asks from the gloom.

"David!" Velma replies as she sees her missing friend tied to a chair.

"Am I ever glad to see you!" David says. "I've been kidnapped by zombies!"

Turn the page.

"There's no such thing as zombies, and I can prove it," Velma proclaims. "But there's something about Bushytail Farm that's so valuable that someone is willing to go to desperate measures to get it."

Velma tries to untie her friend. Her hands are slippery from the oily goo and she can barely untangle the knots.

"And I think I've just figured out what it is," Velma announces. "Follow me and I'll show you."

Velma and David sneak out of the room. She leads them deeper down the tunnel until they come to an amazing sight. David gasps!

Velma and David stand at the opening of a cave. There are a dozen short oil derricks inside the cavern. Zombies work the drills.

"There's petroleum oil under Bushytail Farm," Velma says. She holds out her hands covered in dark goo. "This is the clue that solved the mystery. It's crude oil."

"You meddlers!" a voice grumbles.

Turn to page 102.

Velma and David turn to see a zombie behind them! Thinking fast, Velma uses the rope that once bound David and lassoes the creature. She ties a secure knot and pulls off the ghoulish mask.

"Uncle Mel!" David exclaims.

"*Bah*! I was going to force you to sign over the farm's mineral rights. And I would have gotten away with it except for that girl!" Mel confesses.

"Not just any girl, a member of Mystery Inc.," Velma says.

THE END

To follow another path, turn to page II.

Fred hides in an apple tree and watches the zombies wobble to their feet. They lumber across the farmyard toward the orchard. Fred gulps as he realizes that the creatures are heading straight for him!

"Maybe this wasn't such a good plan after all," Fred shivers.

The zombies shamble up to the tree and stand directly below Fred's hiding spot. Then, they disappear!

"Where did they go?" Fred wonders as he leans over and hangs upside down from the branch. "Wait. There's something strange about the tree trunk."

Fred flips down to the ground to take a closer look.

"There's a doorknob on this tree trunk! It must be a secret entrance, but to what?" Fred says. He grasps the knob and opens the door.

Fred discovers that the trunk of the apple tree is hollow.

Turn the page.

Inside, a ladder leads down into a deep shaft. There is a faint glow of light at the bottom. Fred cautiously climbs down the ladder. He stops before he reaches the base. He hears voices!

"Those Mystery Inc. kids are going to be trouble!" someone says. Fred can't see who it is. "We have to get rid of them or my plan is ruined."

"But boss, they're experts," another voice replies.

"Yeah. I've read about them and their adventures," a third voice states.

Hidden in the shadows of the shaft, Fred clings to the ladder and listens to the conversation. He decides that he has heard enough. It's time to act!

"Don't you know it's rude to talk about someone behind his back?" Fred says as he jumps down from the ladder and steps into the small room.

He sees the zombies and the farm's caretaker standing next to David, who is tied up.

"This isn't a mystery after all," Fred announces as he unties his friend. He points at the caretaker. "You're a disgruntled relative who wants revenge on David. You hired these guys to dress up as zombies to scare people away from Bushytail Farm."

"I told you they were experts!" a zombie says and takes off his mask.

"I had my own plans for the farm," the caretaker grumbles. "But now everything is ruined. I would have gotten away with it except for you."

"My farm is saved, thanks to Mystery Inc.!" David declares.

THE END

To follow another path, turn to page 11.

AUTHOR

Laurie S. Sutton has read comics since she was a kid. She grew up to become an editor for Marvel, DC Comics, Starblaze, and Tekno Comics. She has written Adam Strange for DC, Star Trek: Voyager for Marvel, plus Star Trek: Deep Space Nine and Witch Hunter for Malibu Comics. There are long boxes of comics in her closet where there should be clothing and shoes. Laurie has lived all over the world. She currently resides in Florida.

ILLUSTRATOR

Scott Neely has been a professional illustrator and designer for many years. Since 1999, he's been an official Scooby-Doo and Cartoon Network artist, working on such licensed properties as Dexter's Laboratory, Johnny Bravo, Courage the Cowardly Dog, Powerpuff Girls, and more. He has also worked on Pokémon, Mickey Mouse Clubhouse, My Friends Tigger & Pooh, Handy Manny, Strawberry Shortcake, Bratz, and many other popular characters. He lives in a suburb of Philadelphia and has a scrappy Yorkshire Terrier, Alfie.

GLOSSARY

banister (BAN-is-ter)—the handrail that runs along a staircase

counterfeit (KOUN-tur-fit)—something that is fake, but looks like the real thing

derrick (DER-ik)—a tall, tower-like frame that holds the machine that drills oil wells

ghoul (GOOL)—an evil spirit or ghost, something that looks disgusting and death-like

inheritance (in-HER-i-tuhns)—the money or property that are given to a person after someone dies

investigate (in-VES-tuh-gate)—to search in detail, to search for information about something

meddle (MED-uhl)—to get in the way or to become involved in someone else's business

patent (PAT-uhnt)—a legal document that gives the inventor of an item the only right to make and sell it

pavilion (pu-VIL-yuhn)—an open building that is used for shelter, recreation, or exhibits

quaint (KWAYNT)—pretty or charming

reputation (rep-yuh-TAY-shuhn)—other people's judgment of something's quality or character

revenge (ri-VENJ)—the act of getting back at someone for harming you or someone you care about

YOU CHOOSE JOKES!

YOU CHOOSE which punch line is funniest!

What is a zombie farmer's favorite vegetable?
a. Head of lettuce.
b. Head of cabbage.
c. Head of Farmer Brown.

Why don't zombies like to eat dancers?
a. Dancers give them a ballet-ache.
b. Dancers give them toe-maine poisoning.
c. Dancers make them feel tutu full!

What does a zombie need to make a good farmer?
a. Dead-ication.
b. Ache-ers of land.
c. A skeleton and a head for starters, then he should be able to make his own farmer quite easily.

What did Shaggy say when he first saw the zombie?

a. "That guy looks dead tired!"
b. "I'd shake his hand, but I think it might fall off!"
c. "Why am I afraid of a guy who doesn't have any guts?"

What kind of snack does a zombie farmer like to eat?

a. Chips and human bean dip.
b. Brain muffins.
c. Vanilla ice scream.

Why isn't Velma afraid of zombies?

a. "Zombies are nice — they like me for my brains."
b. She thinks they're super-ghoul!
c. Just like zombies, she likes having friends for dinner.

LOOK FOR MORE...

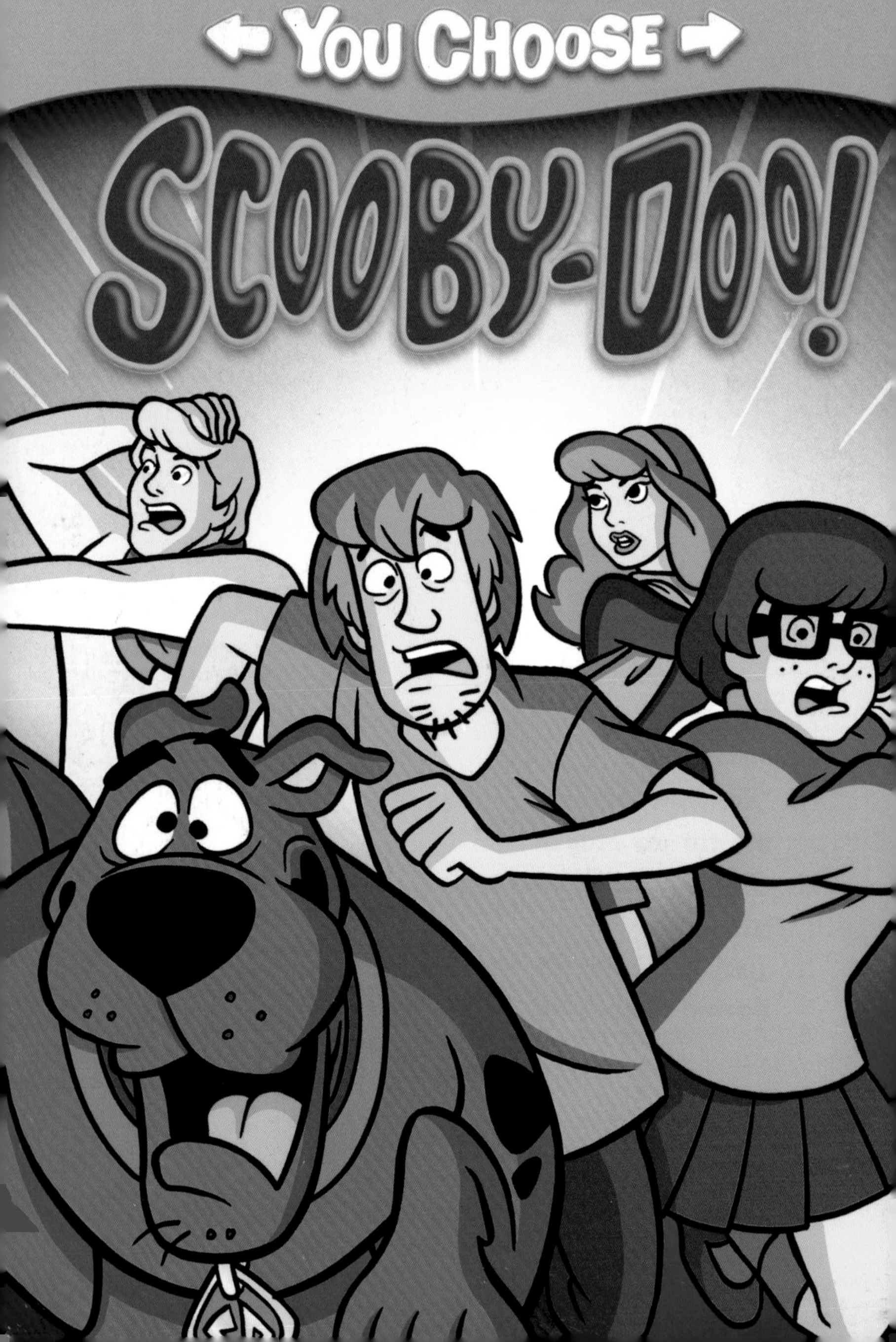

THE CHOICE IS YOURS!